THE EMPEROR AND THE DRUMMER BOY

By Ruth Robbins ✳ Illustrated by Nicolas Sidjakov

PARNASSUS PRESS, BERKELEY, CALIFORNIA

It happened in the French port of Boulogne many years ago.

ENGLAND

The Hague

London

Cologne

Dover

Brussels

BOULOGNE

Frankfort

Amiens

Mainz

Rouen

Rheims

Caen

Paris

Ulm

Alencon

Nancy

Strasbourg

Brest

Fontainebleau

FRANCE
>>>>> 1804 <<<<<

Nantes

Rochefort

Geneva

Milan

Lyon

Bordeaux

Grenoble

Avignon

Toulon

Marseilles

Toulouse

SPAIN

CORSICA

Ships of the Navy lay at anchor in the harbor, and on the shore a regiment of soldiers was encamped. Behind the encampment tall cliffs reached up to form a high plateau.

Here stood the Emperor's pavilion overlooking the sea for miles around.

A quiet channel breeze blew across the quay and into the camp where two young drummers were receiving final instructions from the drum major. "A good practice, mes

petits tambours. Remember, look for my signal before stepping out beside the Admiral. Now, make me proud of you today. Until later, in the square…"

Jean, the younger boy, rubbed his brow. He had worked hard at the drilling—over and over; the roll, the ruffle, the march. But he loved the voice of the drum. A fisherman's son, he had grown with the rhythms of the sea—the surf beating the tilted shore. Only by hard work would he become accomplished with the sticks like his friend Armand. Excitement mounted as he thought of his good fortune; to be drumming with his friend at the grand welcoming of the Emperor to the town of Boulogne.

"He will be here soon, His Imperial Majesty the Emperor Napoleon! Think of it! We will be standing so close to him, Armand! What a great day!"

The older boy, who was taller, with arms too long for his coat sleeves, tried to stifle his eagerness. Was he not a seasoned drummer, having marched with the troops in Hanover? But he, too, felt a tingle of excitement.

"Hurry now, Jean, we must not be late. Is your leather polished? Here, let me button your jacket. Do not fear, you will play well. We will salute His Majesty with the finest rolling of the drums in all of France! Vite! Already people are flooding the roads."

Each fastened his drum to cross strap, each straightened his cap and epaulettes. Together they hurried toward

the town square. Soldiers and sailors in spotless full dress and in strict formation were assembled there. A detachment of the Imperial Horse Guards stood in splendid array; polished swords and shining boots glistened row on row. The air was alive with the ripple of flags, the glitter of harness and saddle. Jean and Armand took their places in the front line of drummers.

Townspeople, farmers, and fishermen crowded the square. Faces watched from the windows and from the rooftops; everyone pushed and stretched for a glimpse of His Majesty the Emperor of France. At last, iron hoof beats sounded on the cobblestone road; then a whisper ran through the crowd. "He comes!"

N apoleon galloped into the square on a white horse followed by his brilliant staff officers and aides-de-camp. "Vive l'Empereur!" A wave of jubilant voices and dancing hands greeted the Emperor. He reined in his horse. Gray coat and white breeches were of fine cloth and easy fit on his compact figure. Only the tricolor cockade adorned his black felt hat. Every man in uniform stood at attention, every officer saluted with pointed sword. And the rolling of the drums swelled to a thundering crescendo that filled the sky and stilled the cheering voices. In the bursting quiet of that moment the two young drummers stepped forward. Heads high, shoulders erect, they escorted Admiral Bruix, commander of the fleet, to Napoleon's side.

The Admiral bowed. Napoleon spoke with clipped accent. His eloquence inspired respect, mingled with fear and affection. "Good day my Admiral, my Colonel, my soldiers and sailors, my citizens of France. This glorious welcome touches me deeply. I am here to inspect personally the fortifications of this great port, to see at first hand my military and naval forces working in unity on land and sea. France is well prepared for great events. I will lead her to victory! Tomorrow my rounds of inspection begin. Now, back to your duties, all." With a wave of his hand, Napoleon rode off in the direction of the pavilion on the cliffs, flanked by eight grenadiers of the Guard. His entourage followed.

At a signal from the drum major, Jean and Armand proudly led the rank and file from the square and through the town. Ta-rum tum *tum*, ta-rum tum *tum*, their drum-

beats paced the marching men behind them. Children strut-
ted along the way. Citizens cheered the lively parade down
the road and back to the camp.

In the dusk, campfires flared along the shore. The beach became a necklace of brilliants around the tall dark cliffs. It was the time for stories and songs and dreams of glory. Jean and Armand flushed with happiness as words of praise fell upon them from the men around their campfire. Out of the shadows stepped the Admiral's aide. His gold braid gleamed in the firelight. Smiling, he turned to the young drummers and said for all to hear, "You have pleased Admiral Bruix by your conduct today. It is his wish that Jean be in his personal service tomorrow, and he permits Armand to accompany sixty soldiers and sailors to a gunboat in the

harbor. You will report to your new assignments after reveille. Now, off to sleep; rest well, a special day awaits you."

A chorus of "good nights" followed Jean and Armand as they ran to their tent nearby. "Can you believe it, Armand? To be serving the Admiral is truly an honor! And you, to see duty on a gunboat! You are in luck, Armand. You will learn the language of the drums at sea. Will you teach me a new flourish when you return? Oh, we will have much to tell each other. I will wait for you on the beach at sundown tomorrow."

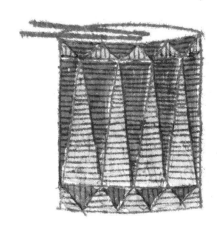

Armand smiled at his friend's lively chatter as they covered their drum heads against the dampness of the night and brushed their red and blue uniforms in readiness for the next day. Then Armand climbed under his blankets with a deep sigh of contentment. "Good night, little Jean."

Jean could not sleep. His thoughts bounded into the

future. He imagined himself a brave son of France in the Grand Army, perhaps the Imperial Guard, riding at the side of his heroic Emperor. He saw himself receiving the order of the Legion of Honor for gallant service to His Majesty. Mother, father, and grandmother would travel from their small village to see him honored. It was hard to wait for tomorrow.

Daybreak came on a gust of wind. Dark mists pushed across the harbor and along the tent-strewn shore. Vapors curled against the cliffs and twisted upward, hugging the rocks, then encircling the pavilion above. Napoleon, standing in his glass-enclosed council chamber, looked out across the channel where, in fine weather, the white cliffs of England could be clearly seen. Through his telescope he scanned the Boulogne harbor. Frigates, bombketches, prams, corvettes, shallops, gunboats: the French Flotilla was a majestic sight before him.

On the wall behind the Emperor hung a large map of the channel coast, with every fortress, every embattlement, every ship's position shown. He studied the map, missing no detail, then returned to his view of the harbor. The drumming of reveille sounded from the camp. Men began to move, like tiny flecks, along the quay and the roadsteads. Two gunboats maneuvered beyond the rocks; all other vessels floated at anchor. The bare masts and shrouds of the ships swayed with the wind, back and forth, like rows of tired skeletons.

Napoleon turned abruptly from the window, picked up his whip, put on his black cocked hat, and left the pavilion. To his officers awaiting him he gave brief, precise instructions for the day. "Come, Roustan," he said to his devoted companion, "we have a morning's ride ahead." Setting spurs to their horses, they descended the cliff toward camp.

Riding through the camp, Napoleon spoke to an officer of the Marine. "Captain, here is a message for Admiral Bruix: I wish to review the fleet on my return from inspection of the land defenses. Have all ships quit their moorings and take positions on the open sea. It is urgent that these

maneuvers be carried out exactly. I expect all to be ready against my return." Having given this order, he rode away.

The captain acted directly and related Napoleon's message to the Admiral. Looking first at the sky, then at the restless waves, Admiral Bruix replied calmly, "I respect

the Emperor's wishes but the barometer falls and there may be no review today." Jean, at his post nearby, heard the Admiral's reply and saw the shocked faces of the men present. Everyone knew that the Emperor's wish was law.

The drummer boy looked out at the ships turning on their anchor chains. His eyes searched for the place where forty gunboats were stationed. Armand was on one of the gunboats, and overhead clouds mounted and darkened a pale sky. Jean smelled the salt-blown air. A storm coming? No fisherman would be out in those waters, he thought. Surely His Majesty would see the danger of reviewing the fleet in this uncertain weather.

Wind hummed through the tent ropes all that morning as Bruix and his staff kept close watch over the fleet. Napoleon would be returning soon. The Admiral looked often at the barometer and saw the mercury shrink steadily in the hollow tube. He was clearly worried. "A storm is approaching this harbor," Jean heard him murmur. "I cannot endanger the lives of those good men." The boy's anxious eyes studied the grave face of the Admiral. Lightning flickered on the horizon. What would his decision be?

A messenger burst in upon them. "His Majesty the Emperor has returned and is now at the north signal point. He wishes to see you, sir, *immediately*." Bruix and his officers departed at once to obey the summons. Jean hurried with them. His body stiffened as he saw the Admiral ap-

proach the Emperor. The two men stood, wind whirling around them, each with steady gaze upon the other.

"Admiral, did you not receive my message that I desire to review the flotilla at sea?"

"I received your message, Majesty."

"How comes it, Admiral, that you have not carried out my instructions?" asked the Emperor in shrill tone.

"Sire," replied Bruix, courteously but firmly, "a terrible storm is brewing, as you can well see. I cannot uselessly imperil the lives of so many brave fellows."

Napoleon's voice exploded like cracking thunder. "Sir, I alone assume responsibility for those men, and for the consequences! Admiral, obey my orders!"

"Sire, I shall *not* obey."

"Monsieur, you are an insolent fellow!" And Napoleon, whip in hand, advanced toward the Admiral with a threatening gesture. Bruix, stepping back, gripped his sword-hilt.

"Have a care, Sire," said he, turning deathly pale.

The men surrounding this scene became frozen with fright: the will of Napoleon, Emperor of France, had been challenged! The enraged Emperor stood motionless for a moment; then he flung down his whip, dismissed Bruix, ordered the Vice-Admiral to carry out his command, and stalked away.

Jean, dazed and confused, felt a tap on his shoulder and heard the Admiral's aide whisper, "You will no longer

be needed to serve the Admiral today." Then he was off. The drummer boy watched the semaphore signal the fleet to lift anchor and prepare for maneuvers. Out on the ships every seaman and soldier did his duty. Sails whipped unfurled, gunboat crews took up their oars. Which gunboat was Armand's? What was he doing now?

What followed was everything Admiral Bruix had feared. All the winds in the world came rushing on that harbor. Thunder roared from the heavens like the rolling of a thousand drums. Lightning pierced the clouds in staccato flashes. Rain pounded down from the black sky. And the vessels danced: a helpless, turbulent dance, given up to the furies of the storm. Sails ripped, lines snapped, and the ships foundered. Men from all sections of the camp now hurried down to the beach and Jean was caught up in the surge. Sand biting his face, he stumbled toward the shore where the small dark silhouette of the Emperor could be seen.

Napoleon saw the tragedy unfold. Head bent against the wind, arms crossed, he paced the water's edge. His temper drained, a feeling of remorse came over him. He, alone, was responsible for those men and for the consequences.

Jean trudged through the lashing rain, a lonely figure following the Emperor. Sea birds screeched in flight. Suddenly, cries rang out above the gale. Twenty gunboats, each carrying a crew of sixty, crashed against the rocks and men jumped from the splintering boats, helpless and calling for help. "Armand! Armand!" cried Jean. An instant, and Napoleon was wading into the shallows and jumping into a small life boat. "Save those men!" he shouted. "We must save them somehow!" A wave broke over his boat and almost washed him overboard, but many strong hands pulled him to safety on the beach. Fired by such courage, officers, soldiers, sailors, and civilians plunged into the raging waters to the aid of the shipwreck victims.

Slowly men were carried up on the sand; others came wading in through the swirling foam, wounded and exhausted. Many valiant men lost their lives that dreadful day.

The rescue continued, the day grew darker. Napoleon walked the beach. No rest until he knew of every casualty, saw every survivor. "My soldiers are my children," Jean heard him say. Through the stinging rain the boy's eyes strained in one direction—where the gunboats had smashed on the rocks. He ran to each form struggling up the beach. "Have you seen the drummer boy, Armand? He was on one of the gunboats and he is my friend." No one could give Jean a word.

"Tambour, what keeps you here in this foul weather?"

Jean looked up. "I wait for my friend, Armand, Your Majesty. I promised to meet him here at sundown."

Napoleon raised his eyes. He looked long into the face of the storm. Then he spoke slowly. "One cannot command the wind. Come, we wait together."

During the night the storm spent itself. A quiet darkness lay over the harbor, broken only by the sound of boots crunching the wet sand, the call of a rescuer, the sob of a wounded man. All night the Emperor and the drummer boy kept watch—one to give courage and comfort to his men, the other to keep alive the hope of finding his friend.

A wreck-strewn Boulogne Harbor reflected the morning's first light. Jean shivered; cold, wet, fatigued. Napoleon stood like stone, his head bent low on his chest. He moved a hand to the boy's shoulder. "You must get some rest, mon petit. I will keep your vigil." Jean was stirred by these words. But one could not weep before his Emperor, not even at a time like this.

"Thank you, Sire. I cannot rest until Armand returns. I beg of you, let me stay a little longer."

"You are a brave lad and a true friend." The Emperor

nodded, "You may remain."

Jean looked toward the sea — broken ships, drifting timbers. Would he never again see Armand? Would they never again drum together at the head of a parade or lie awake together dreaming of glorious deeds? And as he stared his eyes focused on a spot of color. It was gone. Then he saw it again. He blinked to open his eyes wider. A spot of red and blue. He watched it moving closer with the morning tide. It bobbed gently on a wave. Slowly the red and blue became larger and larger. It took shape. Could it be . . . ?

Yes! A boy floating on a drum.

"Armand! Armand! You are alive! At last you have come!" He ran splashing into the surf. "Look! Armand, it is Jean!"

The boy floating in on the drum lifted his head and waved a weary arm. Jean turned to the Emperor and cried out joyfully, "Your Majesty, my friend Armand is here! Alive! He is coming, there on his drum!"

"A noble drum!" The Emperor Napoleon smiled. "From the sorrowful night a brighter day is born. Jean, Armand, together you will march again for France."

And so it happened in the Boulogne Camp many years ago.

AUTHOR'S NOTE

This story is based on history. The tragic incident of the storm and shipwreck at the port of Boulogne occurred in July 1804. Napoleon's forces, Army and Navy, were assembled along the northern coast of France preparing for the invasion of England which never was launched. The episode is related in books and journals. Constant, Napoleon's head valet, in his Memoirs wrote: "That day I saw a drummer, belonging to one of the vessels, who floated ashore on his drum, as if it had been a raft . . ."